The Wishing Foxes

Margaret Read MacDonald
with Jen and Nat Whitman

Illustrated by Kitty Harvill

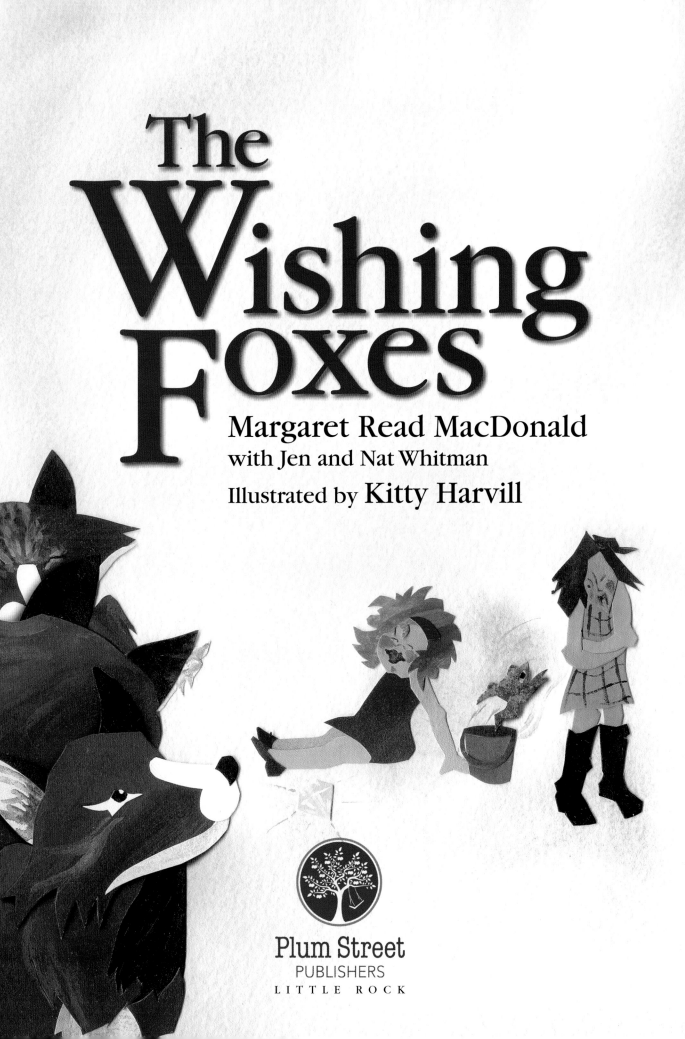

Plum Street
PUBLISHERS
LITTLE ROCK

For Tilda, Delia, and Murray,
who know how to have a lovely, lovely day!
– Granny Mac

For Christoph, who makes every day a lovely, lovely day.
– KH

Copyright © 2017 by Margaret Read MacDonald
Illustrations copyright © 2017 by Catherine Harvill

Published 2017 by Plum Street Publishers, Inc.,
2701 Kavanaugh Boulevard, Suite 202, Little Rock, Arkansas 72205
www.plumstreetpublishers.com
Book design by Charlie Ross

First Edition
Printed in South Korea by Four Colour Print Group, Louisville, Kentucky
10 9 8 7 6 5 4 3 2 1 HB (ISBN 0-978-1-945268-01-4)
LIBRARY OF CONGRESS CONTROL NUMBER: 2016945960

The paper used in this publication meets the
minimum requirements of the American National Standards
for Information Sciences—
Permanence of Paper for Printed Library Materials,
ANSI/NISO Z39.48–1992.

10/12/2016
67680-0
Printed by We SP Corp., Seoul, Korea

ABOUT THE STORY

Tales of kind and unkind girls are told around the world. Warren Roberts discusses more than 900 variants of Aarne–Thompson Tale Type 480 (The Tale of the Kind and the Unkind Girls) in his book *The Tale of the Kind and the Unkind Girls* (Detroit: Wayne State University, 1958). This particular tale is of "The Heads in the Well" subset of the tale. Roberts found versions from Great Britain, the United States, and Scandinavia in which two girls go for water and encounter three heads who ask them to wash and comb them and lay them down gently. The change from disembodied heads to foxes seems to be an Appalachian invention, and a very good change! Leonard Roberts records a version of the fox variant in his *Sang Branch Settlers: Folksongs and Tales of a Kentucky Mountain Family* (Austin and London: University of Texas Press for the American Folklore Society, 1974).

When we tell this story, we sing Bess's and Tess's songs to the tune of "Skip to My Lou."

O nce there was a woman
who had two daughters,
Bess and Tess.
Now Bess spoke kindly to
everyone she met and treated
folks real nice,
but Tess spoke harshly to
everyone and treated
folks badly.

One day, the mother asked Bess,
"Would you go down to the Well-at-the-
End-of-the-World and fetch me some water?"

So Bess started off down the road singing,
"Going to the Well-at-the-End-of-the-World.
What a lovely, lovely day!"

Pretty soon she heard a noise . . . GRRRR.
She turned a corner and . . .

There was a great **big old BEAR!**

GRRRR!

Bess just smiled.
"Good morning, Bear, I see you're feeling grumpy this morning.
I'm going to the
Well-at-the-End-of-the-World.
Would you let me pass, please?"

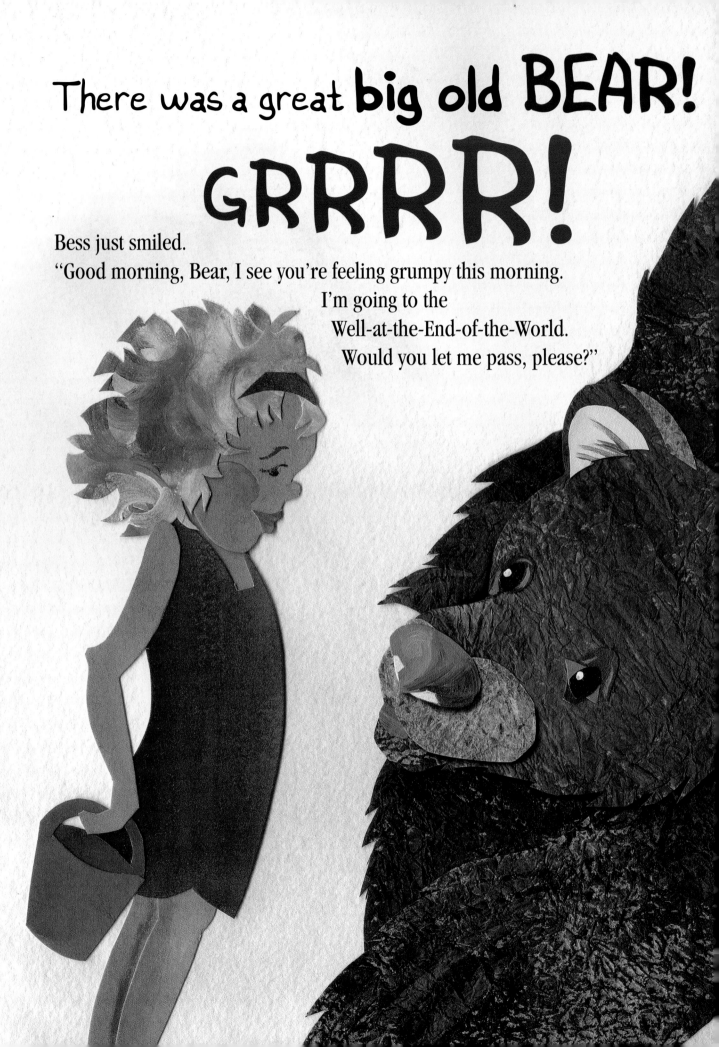

The bear backed off.
"Girl, you just spoke kindly to me.
No one ever speaks kindly to me.
They always holler at me and
shoot guns in my direction.
Why, sure, I'll let you pass."

Bess went on . . .

"Going to the Well-at-the-End-of-the-World.
What a lovely, lovely day!"

She turned a corner and . . .

RAAARR!
MOUNTAIN LION

There was a big right in the middle of the road.

"Good morning, Mountain Lion.
I see you're feeling grumpy this morning.
I'm going to the Well-at-the-End-of-the-World.
Would you let me pass, please?"

The mountain lion stepped back.

"Girl, you spoke kindly to me.
Nobody ever speaks kindly to me.
They all just holler at me and
throw rocks.
Sure, you can pass."

She went on down
the road singing,

"Going to the
Well-at-the-End-of-the-World.
What a lovely, lovely day!"

She turned a corner and . . .

UNH! UNH! UNH!

WILD BOAR

There was a mean old
trying to scare her off.

Bess just smiled.
"Good morning, Boar.
I see you're feeling
grumpy this morning.
I'm going to the
Well-at-the-End-of-the-World.
Would you let me pass, please?"

"Girl, nobody ever speaks kindly to me.
They always call me a smelly, stinky old thing
and kick me.
Of course you may pass."

Bess came to the
Well-at-the-End-of-the-World,
and there were
three little foxes.

"A girl! A girl!
Here comes a girl!"

The first little fox jumped up.
"Pick me up and wash my face
and lay me down right easy."

"What sweet little foxes!"
Bess picked up the first little fox.
She washed its face,
and she laid it down . . . right easy.

The second little fox said,
"Pick me up and wash *my* face
and lay me down right easy."

So Bess picked the second little fox up.
She washed its face,
and she laid it down . . .
right easy.

"Pick me up and wash *my* face,"
called the third little fox,
"and lay me down right easy."

So Bess picked up
the third little fox.
She washed its face,
and she laid it down . . .
right easy.

"Let's all make wishes for this kind girl,"
said the three little foxes.

The first little fox said,
"I wish . . .
Whenever she opens her mouth to talk
gold will fall out on the floor."

The second little fox said,
"I wish . . .
Whenever she sneezes
diamonds will fall out of her nose."

The third little fox said,
"I wish . . .
Whenever she washes her face
her kindness will shine and shine."

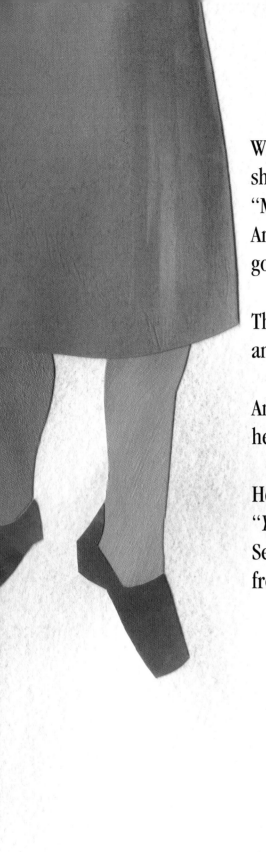

When Bess got back home,
she called out to her mother.
"Mother, I got the water . . ."
And when she opened her mouth to speak,
gold fell out of her mouth.

Then Bess sneezed –*"Achoo!"*–
and diamonds came out of her nose.

And when she washed her face,
her kindness did shine and shine.

Her mother turned to Tess.
"*You* hurry down to that well.
See if you can get some presents
from those foxes too."

So Tess took the bucket and
started down the road, grumping . . .

"Going to the Well-at-the-End-of-the-World.
Everybody get out of my way!"

GRRRR!

There was that great big old **BEAR**,
trying to scare her off.
"Out of my way, you ugly old BEAR!"
Tess whacked at it with her bucket.

GRRRR!

That bear jumped at her,
and she had to run to get away,
but she called back,
"Going to the Well-at-the-End-of-the-World.
You'd better get out of my way!"

RAAARR!

There was the
**MOUNTAIN
LION!**

"Get out of here,
you big old LION!"
Tess whacked at it
with her bucket.

RAAARR!

That Lion jumped at her,
and she had to run to get away.
She shouted,
"Going to the Well-at-the-End-of-the-World.
You'd better get out of my way!"

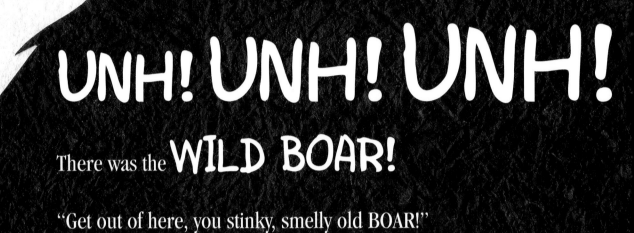

UNH! UNH! UNH!

There was the WILD BOAR!

"Get out of here, you stinky, smelly old BOAR!"
Tess kicked it with her boots.

That Wild Boar jumped at her, and she had to run to get away.

"Going to the Well-at-the-End-of-the-World.
You'd better get out of my way!"

Tess stomped on down
the road and came to the
Well-at-the-End-of-the-World.

"Girl! Girl! Here comes a girl!"

"Pick me up and wash my face
and lay me down right easy,"
said the first little fox.

Here's where I get my presents,
thought Tess.

She snatched up that first little fox.
She sloshed water into its face.
She slung it back onto the ground.

Eeek!
squeaked the little fox.

"Pick me up and wash *my* face
and lay me down right easy,"
said the second little fox.

Tess snatched up that second little fox.
She sloshed water in its face.
She slung it back onto the ground.

Eeek!
"That hurt!"

The third little fox was getting nervous.
"Pick me up and wash *my* face
and lay me down right easy . . . *Please*."

Tess snatched that little fox up.
She sloshed water in its face.
She slung it back onto the ground.

Eeek!

"Let's all make wishes
for this unkind girl,"
said the three little foxes.

The first little fox said,
"I wish . . .
Whenever she opens her mouth to talk
toads will hop out."

The second little fox said,
"I wish . . .
Whenever she sneezes
corn will come out of her nose."

The third little fox said, "I wish . . .
Whenever she washes her face
her meanness will show right there."

When Tess got back home her mother asked,
"Did you get the water?"

"Yes, I did . . . "

But when she opened her mouth to speak . . .
toads hopped out.

Then she sneezed –*"Achoo!"*–
and corn fell out all over the floor.

And when she washed her face . . .
her meanness showed right there.

So after that,
Bess went for water
and Tess stayed home
until she learned how to treat folks right.

Fact is, if you are kind . . .
kindness just comes right back to you.